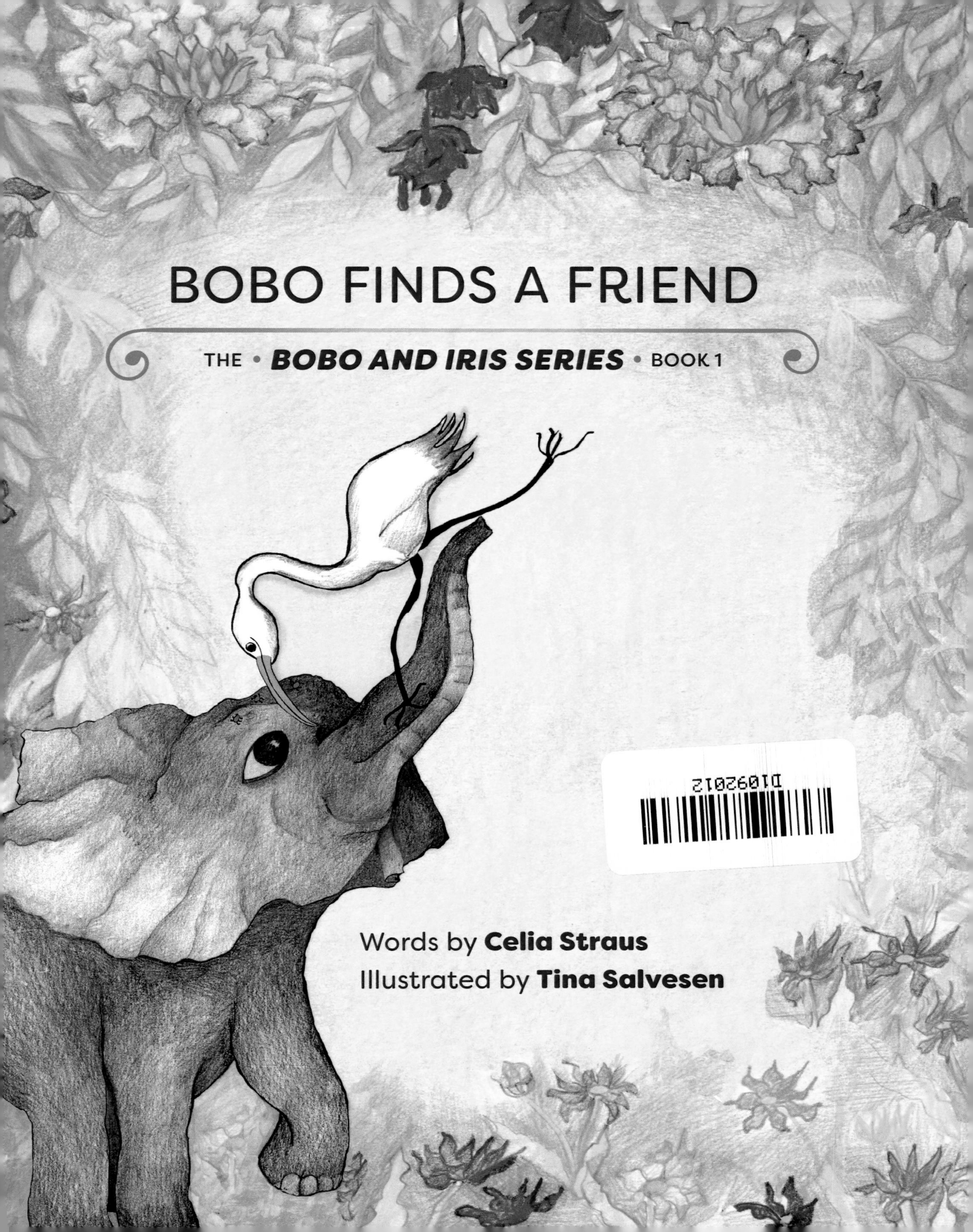

BOBO FINDS A FRIEND

THE • ***BOBO AND IRIS SERIES*** • BOOK 1

Words by **Celia Straus**
Illustrated by **Tina Salvesen**

Published: 2021 by Leschenault Press.

ISBN: 978-1-922670-08-3 - Paperback Edition.
ISBN: 978-1-922670-09-0 - E-Book Edition.

Cover design and interior layout by Krysta Maria Micallef of www.xorxcreative.com from original illustrations by Tina Salvesen.

Reach Celia Straus
Instagram @CeliaStraus
Website www.zoerose.us

Reach Tina Salvesen
Twitter @Tina_Salvesen
Instagram @TinaSalvesen
Website www.tinasalvesen.com
Website www.zoerose.us

THIS BOOK IS DEDICATED

to our wondrous grandchildren

BoBo lived with his elephant family
on the vast plains of Africa.

When his mommy stroked him with her trunk
or sang him sweet lullabies BoBo was
the happiest baby ever.

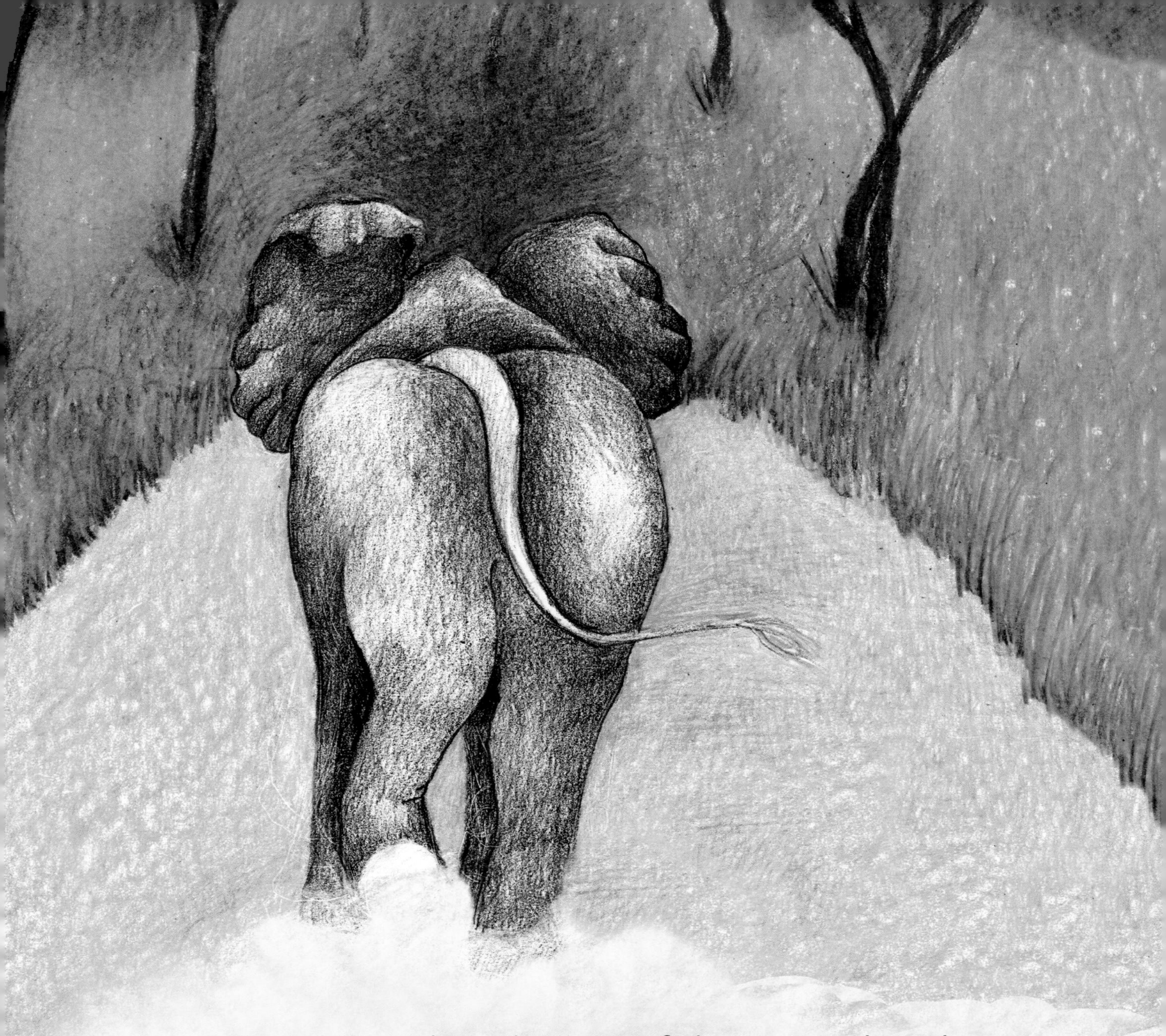

One sunny day, the two of them wandered away from the herd to find a watering hole. Suddenly, they heard a scary sound.

Mommy whispered fiercely,
“BoBo, run! Hide!”

BoBo ran as fast as his short legs could take him.

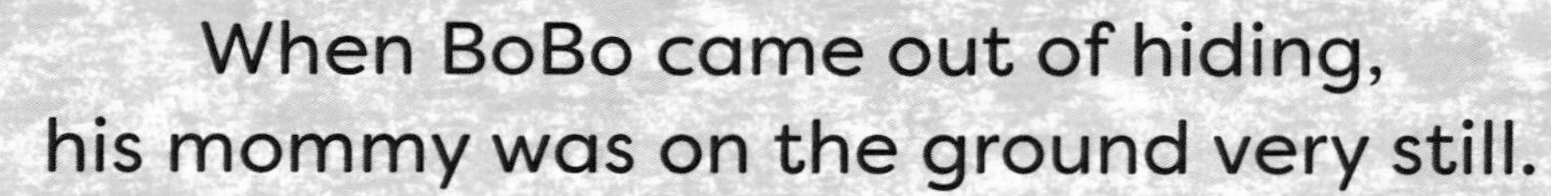

When BoBo came out of hiding,
his mommy was on the ground very still.

"Mommy!"
he cried, but she did not answer.

BoBo huddled
close to her side.

He felt scared,

sad,

and oh

so alone.

A large green jeep rumbled up and four men gently lifted him into the back.

They drove over dusty roads to a place called The Elephant Sanctuary.

They gave BoBo a cozy blanket to keep him warm
and safe, yet his heart still ached because
he missed his mommy.

An elephant named Kindani, waved her trunk and called
to him, but BoBo wouldn't go over to her because
he was shy and afraid of strangers.

He walked into the deep
green forest filled with flowering trees.

His head drooped with unhappiness
as he stared at the forest floor.

Suddenly, a voice screeched

“Watch out!
You’re gonna bump into this treeeeee!”

BoBo hit his head so hard that he fell back on his bottom just in time to see a big white bird flapping wildly above him.

"Are you okay?"
said the bird, landing
on Bobo's foot, her neck stretching
into a squiggle shape.

"Whoops!" she exclaimed.
*"My neck always does that
when I'm excited.*

So, what's your name?"

"*BoBo,*" he said, starting to cry.

"*What's wrong?*" asked the bird.

"*I lost my mommy,*" he sobbed.

The bird hopped to the ground and exclaimed, "*Lost your mommy? Of course, you feel awful.*"

"*But you're going to be okay, I promise. Now take a deep breath and flap your ears.*"

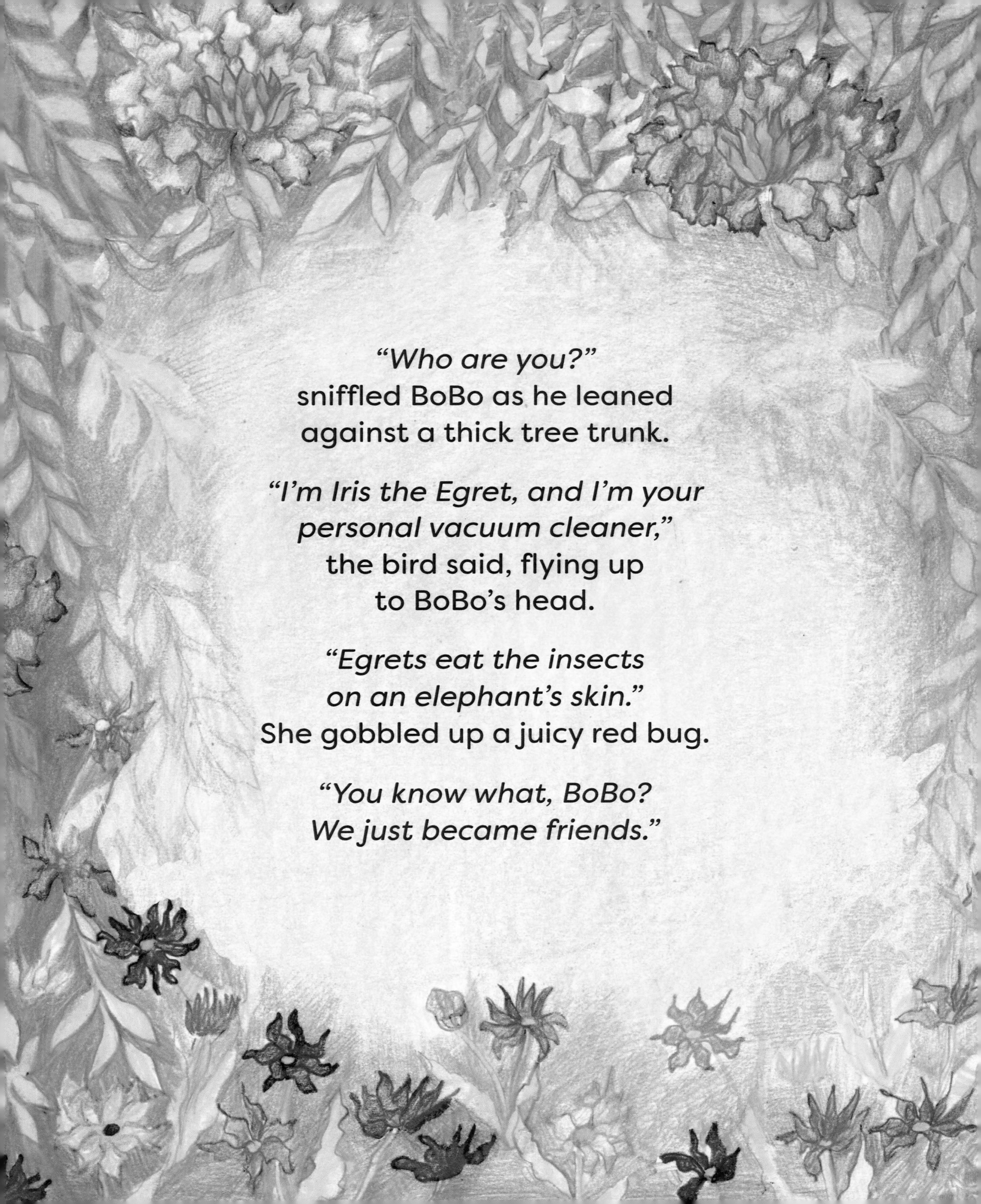

"Who are you?"
sniffled BoBo as he leaned
against a thick tree trunk.

"I'm Iris the Egret, and I'm your
personal vacuum cleaner,"
the bird said, flying up
to BoBo's head.

"Egrets eat the insects
on an elephant's skin."
She gobbled up a juicy red bug.

"You know what, BoBo?
We just became friends."

Bobo knelt on his front feet.
"What's a friend?" he asked.

"I will explain it when you are upright,"
Iris replied. *"It's hard to hold a conversation
with your bottom."*

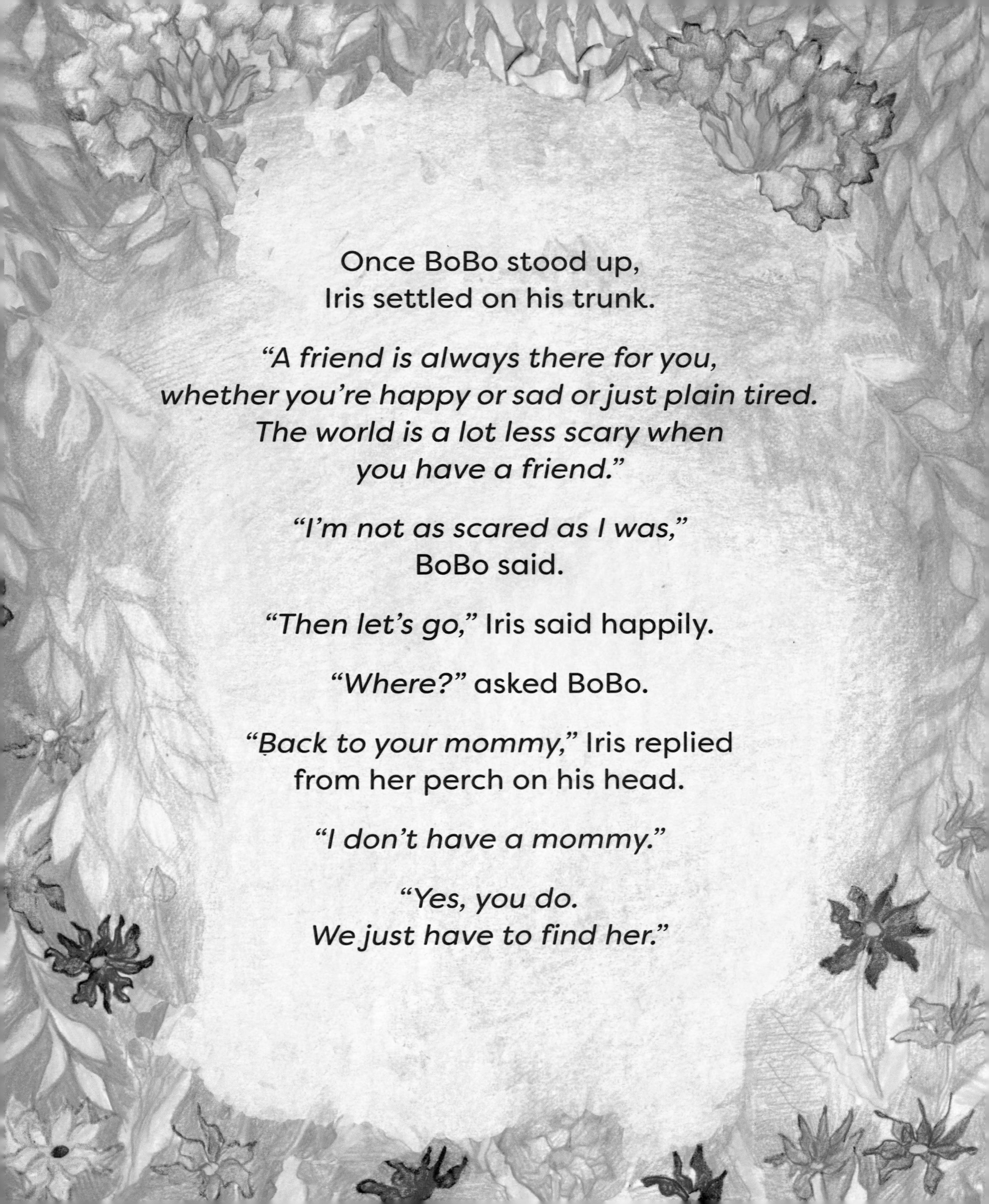

Once BoBo stood up,
Iris settled on his trunk.

"A friend is always there for you, whether you're happy or sad or just plain tired. The world is a lot less scary when you have a friend."

"I'm not as scared as I was," BoBo said.

"Then let's go," Iris said happily.

"Where?" asked BoBo.

"Back to your mommy," Iris replied from her perch on his head.

"I don't have a mommy."

"Yes, you do. We just have to find her."

When they reached the sanctuary, BoBo asked,
"Which mommy is mine?"

"Maybe that elephant waving her trunk at you," said Iris.

"Do you think she wants to be my mommy?" asked Bobo.

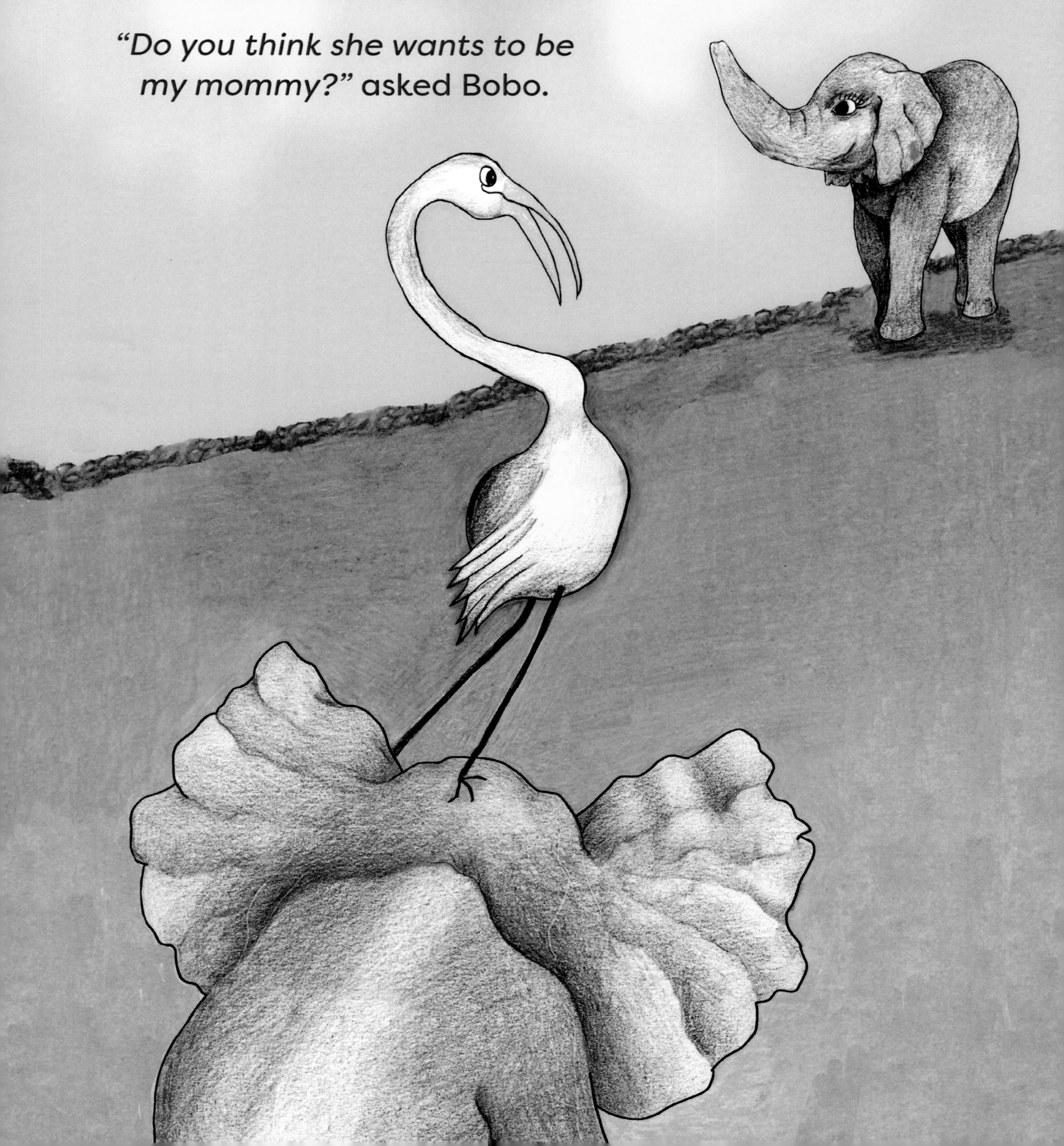

"What's your name little one?"
called Kindani.

Iris pecked his head gently
"Answer her," she whispered.

"My mommy named me BoBo,"
he said timidly.

Kindani wound her long trunk
around him and hugged him close.
"Then that's what I'll call you."

BoBo felt warm all over
and he knew he was loved.